MOUSE CODE

J-FIC

MOUSE CODE

JOEL THURTELL

HARDALEE PRESS

Published by Hardalee Press
11803 Priscilla Lane
Plymouth, MI 48170

Cover and interior design by Maya Rhodes

Library of Congress Control Number: 2009906763

Thurtell, Joel Howard

ISBN 9780975996942

FOR ABE

TROUBLE WITH MORSE

A long time ago, when I was a boy, I had a big, gray two-dial radio in my bedroom. When the lights were off and everyone else was asleep, I would creep out of bed and switch my radio on. The dials would glow like big amber eyes as I roved up and down the shortwave bands. In the stillness of the night, headphones clamped over my ears so my mom and dad and brothers wouldn't hear, I would listen to Morse Code. In the comfort of my little room, I would eavesdrop on coded messages from far-off places. It was exciting. But often, very late, something strange happened to those dits and dahs. My tired brain, it seemed, was twisting the Morse letters into characters that didn't make sense.

In those days, I spent every Saturday afternoon in Homer Crouch's radio shop. Homer Crouch was my guide, the man who encouraged me to study for an amateur radio license so I could send radio signals and talk to people. He ran a radio repair shop in our town. While his technicians were busy fixing police radios, I was allowed to use the shop tools, building small radios of my own.

As time went on, my confusion about Morse Code bothered me more and more. Homer Crouch was the only person who might understand, but he wasn't the easiest person to come to with a problem. In our little town, he was known as something of a crank. People avoided him. Behind his back, they made

jokes about him. Smart, yes; a radio genius, yes, people said, but Homer Crouch is a hard man to get along with. His tongue was sharp and his patience was short.

He was tall and stoop-shouldered, with oily white hair that stood away from his head in broad wings. He looked just like what you'd think a crotchety old inventor would look like. Well, that's what he was. Before anyone else did it, Homer Crouch put radios in the police cars and fire trucks in our little town. It was wonderful to have police radio in the 1920s. Too wonderful, maybe. The polite people in town called Homer "eccentric." I heard worse. My friends would say, "He's a mean son of a gun, a grumpy old coot – how can you stand him?"

Homer did make a bad impression. With a well-chawed cigar stub clamped between his yellow teeth, the old man would rant and rave at the fireman who blew up a transmitter by sending a signal without an antenna.

Now, by the time I knew him, they were making fancy two-way radios, and he no longer built the radios he installed. He fixed radios built in factories. That was why they had to be fixed, because they weren't made with care, he grumbled. He had no patience for engineers who dreamed up circuits that didn't work the way he thought they should.

"Idiots!" he would snarl, often using harsher words. He seemed to like the sound of ornery. If the phone rang, he'd pick it up and growl, "This is the Grouch!"

I wondered if, maybe, he really enjoyed being known as an ogre. No, it would not be easy to talk to Homer Crouch. But there really was nobody else in town who knew about radios. About RADIO. I waited until the repairmen were out of the shop, then screwed up my nerve.

"Mr. Crouch," I said. "Have you ever had your mind play a trick on you late at night listening to Morse Code? Like hearing a V (. . . -) but thinking it was a B (- . . .)?"

"That's not in your mind," the old man said, shifting the juicy end of a cigar to the other side of his mouth. "And it's not Morse Code, either. Not exactly."

I waited, but he seemed to have forgotten me. He pressed the tip of his soldering gun against the lug of a tube socket.

3

A thin gray curl of smoke rose above his head. Finally, speaking around the stump of that slimy cigar, he announced: "It's Mouse Code."

I captured a snicker, held it, choked it down. Mouse Code! But I was puzzled. Homer Crouch was not a whimsical man. He didn't joke around.

Mouse Code?

He continued to work, aiming the beam of a flexible desk lamp into the chassis of the two-way radio. "You hear it mostly late at night – that's when the mice like to work. But if there's trouble, you'll hear them no matter what time it is."

"Mice?" I said. "Mice have radios?"

"Well, sure they do," Homer Crouch said. "Of course, they didn't invent radio. Neither did I. You might say they borrowed the idea. And the parts, for that matter. Stole them, some would say. But they did invent Mouse Code. They had to."

"Mouse Code? Why not just use Morse Code?"

The old man leaned back and cracked a smile. "Why? To keep me from eavesdropping."

"You?"

There was a glitter in the old radioman's eye now. I was skeptical.

"How do you know all this?" I said.

"Easy," he replied. "I learned Mouse Code."

DISASTER

Arthur Mouse smelled strong black coffee mixed with the sweet aroma of sizzling bacon long before he saw the hole leading down to Kaiser's Kitchen. For a mouse, smells are signposts. He'd scampered out of his last class at North Field School, picked up 50 copies of the *Rodent Herald* and started delivering newspapers. Kaiser's Kitchen was the last stop on Arthur's paper route.

Arthur pushed through the narrow tunnel purposely dug just large enough to let a mouse or mole or medium-sized rat through, but just as purposely made small enough to keep out prowling foxes and badgers. A jagged piece of rock poked partway up from the floor of the little tunnel – Kaiser Rat's precaution against Slim, the big Blue Racer. It wouldn't stop Slim, but it sure would slow him down. Finally, the little pas-

sage widened into a broad vault – Kaiser Rat's dining room.

Before he reached the big room, Arthur could hear a loud discussion. Kaiser, a potbellied river rat with a sharp, spade-like chin beard, was a rat of many and lengthy words. He'd taken Latin at Groundhog Tech – one semester, which he failed – in an attempt to give his conversation what he thought was a scholarly polish.

Kaiser Rat was grilling fat, yellow kernels of corn on a woodstove and listening to the low murmur of animals talking and chomping on corn. The creatures were unsettled about the things going on in the world above their heads.

Suddenly, Kaiser's voice rose above the din. "Why did I pick, I say, why did I selectionate this here locashamon for my place of business? Good reason, dear rodentmen and rodentwomen. This here locashamon is in the flats, my friends, where you can reach my locus operandibus with facilitude. With facilimitude! Hence and orgo I'm not about to move my commercibus just because some old field mouse says Kaiser's ain't sino dangerabo," Kaiser Rat declaimed. "Safety, gentlemicem, that is Kaiser's middle moniker. Why, North Field has not felt the scimitar (by which I mean a plow) in nigh onto 30 annuals. It's nice and flat and smacko in the middle – which is to say the centralitude — of all yer finest field mouse subdivisimons. Why, there's hardly a mouse who is not at least tempterated to malinger into my environs on his way to the gleanings. I tell you, dear mice, rats, moles and voles, irregarterless, the business of Kaiser Rat has not been better."

"All of that may be very true," said Roger Mole. "Yet you have to admit, Kaiser, that the plows have been ripping soil closer and closer to home. Last spring a whole clan of shrews were turned out of their den without any notice at all. I saw it myself. The plows they have today are bigger and dig deeper and they're pulled by giant coughing monsters, not horses. We can't stop it. The day when a couple of barn rats could spook a dumb draft animal is gone, Kaiser. Maybe Hannibal Mouse was right to move to the slope."

"Hannibal Mouse!" Kaiser sneered. "Irregarterless, I tell you, Hannibal Mouse is a broken-down, swaybacked, pomposified old field marshal who's lost his nerve and rodent fortitudimitude. He may have duped and trumped and bulldozidated the owls into a truce and treaty, but that was way back when. He might have trumpelated the foxes with his Trojan hen, but that was nigh onto nigh on. Where is the old impostapator

now? He's desertimated us! Who ever heard of a field mouse living on a hill? It's totalamally, unalterabelly and irrebroccoli contraridary to Instinct."

"Well," said Roger Mole, who enjoyed a good argument and Kaiser Rat's goofy lingo more than the roasted corn on Kaiser's short menu, "well, Kaiser, you have to admit he's working for a noble cause. He wants to warn us when the tractors are coming."

Kaiser Rat turned a row of corn kernels over, exposing their blackened undersides. "Noble! Noble! Noble is as noble does! His causus noble? His causus is dumb. Proven poppycockidock. Those flags of his didn't work, did they? What about that telescopidity? Why, he couldn't see the signal mice wiggle-wagging in the fog. Not even a sewer rat could run the news with more celery, celeritude, celeritato, than one of those field-killer mechanified monstrositudes. No, if you ask me, Roger, signalizing is Hannibal's pretexto for what I call a coward's getting when the getting's good. He's betrayed all North Field. Simple as that."

"Ah, Kaiser," mumbled a timid house mouse. "I think you'd better calm down. You're shaking."

"Shaking! I'm not either s-s-shaking!" said Kaiser Rat. But he looked at the paw holding the spatula and saw that he was indeed trembling. What's more, his wood cookstove was shaking, too. His entire dining room was shivering.

"It's an earthq-q-q-quake!" screeched the mole.

A long explosive din filled the chamber. Dust rose from the floor, pieces of dirt fell from the walls and ceiling. Kaiser Rat's mouth was going, but you couldn't hear him. He was pointing toward the hallway where the mole was scurrying for the outdoors.

Suddenly, something hard, sharp and shiny punched through the ceiling.

"Scim-m-mitar!" screeched Kaiser.

"The plow!" shouted Roger Mole.

A long, deadly blade carved a great groove in the floor, knocking tables and cookstove aside. The earth heaved. Mice, rats, moles all were tossed into the air. Then, just as quickly as it had come, the blade was gone.

Kaiser Rat was lying on his back, panting. "I'm dead! Perished! Oblitimerated! Destructified!" he groaned.

Arthur groaned, too. Sunlight stabbed through the dust. Arthur Mouse stood up and brushed dirt from his fur. The hallway was blocked by a huge chunk of sod, but he simply climbed out through a wide gap in the wall. As he stood in the open, Arthur looked along a neat, freshly made furrow. The long grass and scrub brush so familiar to the field mice had vanished. At first, all he could see was fresh dirt everywhere.

Then, here and there, soil began to move as mice dug out of their premature graves. Salvaging what they could from their burrows, they stood in small knots, talking quietly.

"My house – my home!" sobbed a mouse, waving her tail frantically as she tried to signal her eight children to follow her — but where to?

A black shadow flitted across the moist soil. Arthur looked upward. Shorty the Red-tailed Hawk was soaring overhead, looking for a free lunch.

"Run! Cover!" yelled Arthur, pointing to the sky with his long tail.

But there was nowhere to hide.

From far off, Arthur could hear the faint chugging of a tractor. North Field had been plowed.

SOMETHING MISSING

Homer Crouch was a young man in those days. While his hair, as always, stood out from the sides of his head like wings, it was a greasy blond, not yet white. He lived alone in an old farmhouse beside a meadow that widened into a broad field. It was known to the mice as North Field, and though it had once been farmed, it now had lain fallow for years.

At night, Homer worked for the railroad. He was a telegraph operator. After a long night of sending and receiving clickety-clack Morse, he would come home at dawn too wound up to sleep right away. Instead of going to bed, he invented.

During the long nights while he was telegraphing for the railroad, odd things began to happen back in that farmhouse of his. First it was a spool of thin-gauge wire that turned up missing. Homer looked high and low and never did find that wire. He eventually gave up looking for an entire box of spare vacuum tubes that had vanished. There were other things, too, but most perplexing was the strange behavior of his thick manual called *The Radio Amateur's Handbook*. Each morning Homer would come home tired, but his mind would be thinking about his latest invention, which was a radio that would transmit and receive voices and fit in a car's glove compartment. Doesn't sound like much now, but it was a big deal in those days. Anyway, he would come home and there would be the *Handbook*, not lying spine out in the bookshelf where he knew he'd left it, but sitting open, propped at an angle for easier reading. Who was doing this?

Homer was intrigued by this new problem – this was a mystery. Who would want to know how to build a primitive one-tube shortwave receiver? Or a simple, one-tube transmitter?

Homer soon connected the loss of radio parts to the book's peculiar behavior. Yes, indeed! The missing parts matched up with components the *Handbook* called for in these projects.

Well, well. Now he knew *what*, but he was stymied by the question: *Who?*

RADIO PLANS

Hannibal Mouse woke from his mid-afternoon nap. He was sore. There was a crick in his tail. The muffled roar from the engine room had finally broken through his slumber. He'd come home at dawn exhausted. Field mice are professional gleaners, of course, but for some time, Hannibal had been picking through what for a mouse was more than an odd field. It was – again for a mouse – a revolution in thinking. But the long nights studying radio circuits from Homer Crouch's book, then the days of lugging parts back to Stone Mountain, wiring them together to make radios that worked – all of this was wearing the old field mouse down.

The crisis had come last night – unexpectedly and shockingly. As he recalled his ordeal, he gave thanks that he was even back in his hole and able to carry on. He'd slept like a boulder. Well, a small one – and his long, gray field mouse tail had bent straight back underneath his furry, white body. The pain reminded him he had more pondering to do. For

his sleeping had not begun back here in the depths of Stone Mountain. Tired out from all the borrowing and building and directing and generating he'd been doing, Hannibal had fallen asleep while reading the radio manual in Homer's house. And he'd been startled awake by the sound of Homer himself coming home and worse, abruptly entering his radio room.

Hannibal's tail had straightened in fright, his fur bristling on his back. Frozen in fear, he had suddenly come alive, urged by Instinct, and bounded behind a curtain. He was sure Homer had seen him. Question was, would the radioman make the connection between a sleeping mouse and missing radio parts?

Now, hours later, he slowly walked out of his sleeping quarters in the deepest end of a long tunnel in Stone Mountain. His way was lit here by a green lightbulb, there by a red bulb, or a blue, and again a red light. The old mouse had scavenged strings of Christmas tree lights from storage in various houses, and they illuminated the lofty caverns of his hillside retreat.

Hannibal Mouse covered his ears as he passed the chamber where a lone model airplane motor screamed its high-pitched shriek. The motor was connected through an ingenious gear reduction system to a child's electric train engine. By turning the locomotive's motor, the little system actually produced electricity.

Electric motors, you see, can work as generators of electricity if, instead of receiving electrical power, they allow their shafts to be turned by some other power. This generator was making electricity for Hannibal Mouse's headquarters on Stone Mountain. A pair of young mice wearing tiny earmuffs sat on the floor. They worked with miniature wrenches taken from toy sets. Parts of another airplane motor lay strewn in front of them. Hannibal Mouse nodded approval at their repair work and moved on.

The Oscillator and Amplifier rooms were quiet and dim, illuminated only by the orange glow of vacuum tubes. Two wires, separated every so often by lengths of pigeon feather, stretched upward and out the mouth of Hannibal Mouse's headquarters. Hannibal Mouse stepped out of the dimness of his hole and peered at the fog. His headquarters was set near the top of a rocky knoll, and he could peer across the tops of dark green spruces and see the long plain of North Field stretching into the distance.

Below his cave, two mice labored at fastening the ends of the double length of wire to the leg of a sparrow. Like the tubes and capacitors and resistors in the underground radio rooms, this wire had been borrowed from Homer Crouch's vast stock of spare radio parts. Homer would never miss it, and to the field mice it was literally a life-and-death matter, as Hannibal knew.

Hannibal planned to set up small sending-and-receiving stations at the edges of North Field. Watchers organized in shifts would report the tractor's operations, as well as sightings of owls, hawks, foxes, weasels and a host of other creatures made by Nature to terrorize mice.

Loaded with Hannibal's homemade feed line, the sparrow lifted off, flapping laboriously under the burden of weight that increased as more wire left the ground. Finding a good stiff breeze higher up, the sparrow soared to the top of a pine.

Two fellow sparrows began attaching the wires to the center of a long wire antenna suspended between three treetops. This was known to radio people as a "Dipole." From his reading, Hannibal had learned that this wire would send out radio waves made by his little transmitters.

Hannibal Mouse looked toward a narrow furrow of matted weeds – this was the mouse trail winding down to North Field. Trudging upward was Arthur Mouse, his young and loyal assistant. Hannibal knew already what Arthur would report – more mice turned out of their homes, chopped to pieces, left prey for lazy, gust-soaring hawks or skulking snakes.

At the moment, though, Arthur Mouse wasn't thinking so much about the calamity below as he was worrying about the things Kaiser Rat had said about the quirky old general. Arthur knew what field mice were saying about Hannibal, too. How the Owl Truce he'd negotiated was a long time ago. The Fox Treaty was still in force, but it was old history, taken for granted. Hannibal had broken the most sacred Field Mouse Canon by moving off North Field. How can you be a field mouse without a field? He'd bucked against everything that Instinct stood for and people were calling him Crazy, Looney Tunes or worse – a Coward who didn't dare face the might of the Iron Rake. And they were beginning to murmur unkind things about those mice and other animals who were loyal to old Hannibal. No, it was not easy for Arthur Mouse to keep visiting his old friend.

But there were still some mice who remembered Hannibal's brilliant service in the Old Days. And there were loyal sparrows and moles who didn't care a corn kernel what mice thought, anyway. They only remembered that those treaties had kept North Field free of predators for many a year.

Arthur approached and began to give his leader a full report of the carnage, but Hannibal silenced him with a wave of his forepaw.

"Arthur," the old general said, "I know what you're going to say before you say it. We don't have time for such grim news. We must labor toward a time when you will not come up to this height with such awful reports. Today you and I will embark on the last part of my plan to deliver Mousekind from the Plague of Plows."

TRAIL OF FEARS

Getting all this homemade radio equipment ready for the emergency at hand would have been a mammoth undertaking for a human being. Think what it must have been like for a mouse. Having assembled his equipment, Hannibal Mouse had left one crucial detail to the very last. His purpose was to signal warnings to residents of North Field. He would need some way of making his transmitters tell his receivers what was happening. Not wanting to complicate things with using voice communication, his idea was simply to turn transmitters on and off to send his messages.

A switch, called a key, would do the trick. But even such a simple concept needed something more. If you were going to telegraph the letters of the alphabet, you would need a separate sound for each letter. Hannibal didn't have this. Yet. But he would not be the first aspiring ham radio operator to procrastinate about learning the Code. Now he needed it badly. And since there was no time to waste making one up, he planned on borrowing that, too.

Where would he get a code? Where else? From Homer Crouch.

But time was precious. The latest depredations of the Iron Plow were a sign that all of North Field might soon be turned under. Hannibal Mouse could not wait until nightfall to steal into Homer's house and take what he needed.

"Arthur," he said, "I have a dangerous, desperate plan, and I need your help. We have to move fast and get this Code upon which our whole plan depends. I want to start training field mice in sending and taking Code this very night. I'm going into the human's house by daylight, this morning. You will be my lookout, but only if you're willing. The risk to both of us is high."

Homer watched Arthur's pointy snout for signs of fear.

"You see, Arthur,..." Homer paused. "Homer Crouch has a Cat."

Also, Hannibal neglected to add, Homer Crouch by now knew something was afoot. For Arthur, though, there was no hesitation. His respect for Hannibal Mouse was so great that any service he could perform was an honor.

Sunlight cut through the fog. Under a bright sky, the two mice began their long scamper down Stone Mountain, with the old field marshal explaining his plan along the way.

A shadow floated across the path in front of them.

"Hawk!" squeaked Arthur Instinctively. He shouldered against Hannibal, and both mice rolled off the path, the old field mouse sputtering, "What? Where?"

Whoosh. Whump. A huge bird with a crimson tail banged into the path, its downspread tufted legs splaying wide from the crash. Swiveling its head left and right, the hawk's dark, glittering eyes picked out the two field mice now shuddering in the cleft of a Scotch pine trunk.

"Tarnation!" fumed the hawk. "Excessive left rudder. Confounded downdraft. Not to mention lice in tail feathers. Not my day." Addressing the mice, he said, "Gentlemice, you evaded me today and have luck to thank. I am truly sorry. From the looks of you, I would have enjoyed a sumptuous breakfast. Next time, I'll have better luck and you'll have worse."

"Better learn to fly," said Hannibal Mouse.

One treaty Hannibal had never managed to negotiate was an armistice with the hawks.

With a scornful look and three wide beats of his wings, the hawk was airborne and climbing, on the lookout for a quick meal.

It was a harrowing occurrence, and both mice now focused on getting to Homer Crouch's house.

"The Cat is an old black-and-white tom," said Hannibal. "At night he sleeps outside under the hood of the car. But when

23

the human comes home in the morning, he lets the Cat in. I have no idea what that Cat does inside during the day because I've always stayed away when it's light."

Two dark-gray blurs sped over the grass, stopping beside a concrete block, part of a house foundation.

"Follow me," whispered Hannibal. He led Arthur along the side of the house, nearly to a corner. There, he pointed to a dark opening, a hole where mortar between two blocks had cracked. Hannibal had worked many hours chipping away to turn the crack into a hole. Promptly and silently, the old field mouse pushed his head, shoulders and finally his hindquarters through the hole. He disappeared in the darkness.

"Follow me," Hannibal's voice came from inside the house. Now, I said that Arthur was a loyal friend, proud to serve Hannibal and the cause of saving Mousedom. But Arthur had other feelings, too. He was a mouse like any other, and the fur on his back was stiffening as he peered into that dark crack. What lay inside was Unknown. He glanced over his shoulder and sniffed the air. All clear. He squeezed through the hole and found himself standing in a dark cavern. Arthur took a step and bumped into Hannibal.

"Easy, easy," said the old mouse.

DID IT WITH MIRRORS

Hannibal Mouse didn't need to worry that Homer Crouch would spot him. That discovery had taken place several days earlier when Homer had found a tuft of fur lying on the open page of a radio book.

Curious, he switched shifts with a friend at the Big Bunk Railroad terminal and stayed home one night. Borrowing from the idea of the periscope, he arranged a series of mirrors so that he could watch the desk where his radios and books were set up without being in the room. Then he waited.

Soon, his patience paid off. A gray-furred old field mouse had poked his head around the corner of Homer's old receiver. The mouse sniffed, turned his head in all directions, and, satisfied that he was alone, boldly walked out and opened a book.

It was a struggle for the little mouse to turn pages, but his reading

25

astonished Homer. For most certainly the mouse was reading. What else could it be? Hannibal stood at the top of the page, left-hand side, and walked rightward to the end of the sentence, then sprinted back left. Pacing in this way, the old mouse walked the sentences to the bottom of the page.

Now, it was one thing for a mouse to read about radio. What, wondered Homer, was this old rodent doing with the knowledge? And suddenly Homer knew. The missing wire, vacuum tubes, capacitors, resistors – it was this old mouse!

Homer left his mirrors in place. He wanted to see more.

BAPTISM

"Follow me. Carefully," whispered Hannibal Mouse. "I've dug pawholds in these blocks, so just put your feet where you see me put mine."

Slowly, in the dark basement, Hannibal Mouse worked his way down the wall. And just as slowly, Arthur Mouse began to follow, paw by paw. But just as he shifted his weight toward his outstretched foreleg, a chunk of mortar crumbled into dust and the young mouse pitched sideways in a steep arc.

Splash! He sank deep into water, to surface chilled and coughing. Thrashing wildly, he hit something hard and slippery.

"Arthur!" Hannibal was staring down at him from his perch halfway up the wall. Homer had set a pan on the concrete floor to catch a pipe drip. Arthur had landed square in the pan of water.

Hannibal leapt from the wall, caught the rim of the pan

with his right forepaw and hung on. He scrambled over the top and spotted Arthur splashing in panic, trying to climb the slippery side of the pan.

"Arthur! Listen to me. Stop flailing. Swim! Easy, easy." Hannibal Mouse crept along the narrow, curved edge of the pan until he was opposite his friend. He swung his hindquarters over the water and directed his long tail towards Arthur. "Grab my tail!" shouted Hannibal.

He winced as Arthur latched on with his teeth. The pain from last night's crick got worse as he lifted. "Hang on!" The old mouse jumped over the side, stopping short of the floor when Arthur's weight snapped his tail taut. Arthur pushed his back legs against the wall of the pan. With Arthur pushing and Hannibal's weight at the other end, Arthur slowly rose. Hannibal swung lower and soon was on the floor, tail and hindquarters aching. Arthur shivered on the rim of the pan.

"Jump down here and I'll find some newspaper," said Hannibal. "You need to dry off. But quietly, quietly," he muttered. "There's a Cat here somewhere."

MOUSE CODE

Arthur's mouth puckered. His nose quivered. "There's Cat stench everywhere!" he said. "Makes me sick."

"Yes, but that's good, Arthur. The Cat lays down so much stink of his own that he can't detect the delicate odor of mouse. He's got to see us to find us."

The young mouse was not so sure. High above, the black knob of Homer Crouch's receiver shone in the dim light that came through a lightly cur-tained window. Hannibal was al-ready climbing the leg of a chair and leaping to the tabletop. By the time Arthur caught up, the old mouse was turning pages. Hard work. Finally, he found what he wanted. It was a chapter headed "Morse Code." Arthur could see the al-

phabet in bold letters. Beside each letter was a symbol of long or short ink lines.

"No time to lose," Hannibal said. "I'll chew from the top, you munch from the bottom. Meet you in the middle. We'll take this page back to Stone Mountain. Tonight we learn the Code."

As Arthur bent down to chomp, something frightful strayed across the corner of his eye. To the side and behind the radio, he saw – a face! A human face. It was staring at him. His little heart pumped faster and faster. How could this be? There was no room back there for a creature the size of a human.

As Arthur stared at Homer Crouch's face in the mirror, it vanished. Then from a loudspeaker on the table came a tone – two sounds.

Beep-BEEEEP.

"A," a man's voice said.

"I'll teach you the Code, boys," the voice continued. "Dit-dah is A."

Cagey old Hannibal. While Arthur sat down and memorized Morse Code from Homer Crouch, the old general hatched a new scheme.

You see, being a martial type of fellow, Hannibal was not thrilled with letting his enemies, or even friends, know what he was thinking. If he was going to send messages by radio, he didn't want outsiders to read his mind. Now, it was nice of this human to teach his new friends Morse Code. But the mice needed a Code that even this helpful human could not understand. Who was to say whether this radioman would be a friend to mice tomorrow? He harbored a Cat, didn't he? For all Hannibal knew, the man might be sending the Iron Rake to ruin the homes of mice. Anyway, from long dealings with owls, hawks, weasels, and badgers, Hannibal knew that the ally of today can easily become tomorrow's archenemy.

While Arthur was learning the Code forward, Hannibal, so to speak, was getting it backward. He slid the page with

Morse Code in front of the mirror and made mental notes on what he saw.

Now an A looked like this: dah dit.

And a B came out dit dit dit dah instead of dah dit dit dit.

Of course, symmetrical letters like K – dah dit dah – came out the same, but it was enough of a shuffle to throw spies and snoops off the track. So thought Hannibal Mouse.

At this point in his tale, Homer Crouch had finished soldering resistors to the tube socket. His soldering iron had cooled off as he'd warmed to his story.

"No, you couldn't call that Morse Code," Homer Crouch told me. "Naturally, I'd set up a second set of mirrors in that room, so I saw every move that sly old mouse made.

"Including," Homer said, "The Invention of Mouse Code."

WHAT HAPPENED TO NORTH FIELD

Homer Crouch laid his soldering gun on the workbench. He stood up, spread his long arms out in a big stretch, and set the stump of a slimy cigar on the edge of a tin ashtray. I was waiting for him to tell me what had happened with Mouse Code and how things had turned out at North Field. I knew the signs – standing up, stretching, cigar on hold – he was getting ready to go home. I was right; he pushed his stool aside, turned, and headed for the door.

"Wait a minute, Mr. Crouch!" I said. "Tell me the ending – please! What happened to Arthur Mouse? Did Hannibal's radio alarm plan work? Did Mouse Code save North Field from the plow?"

"Well, young man," said Homer Crouch, "that's a lot of questions so late in the day. Why, it took me half the after-

noon to tell you how the field mice invented Mouse Code. Do you think I have all evening to tell you about the adventures of Arthur and Hannibal and the Triumph of Mouse Code? Or how Hannibal tricked the humans into signing the Treaty of the Plows?"

"Aha!" I said. "So Mouse Code was a huge success!"

"That, young man, depends on what you mean by 'success.' Those farmers weren't about to stop planting their corn and soybeans. Builders weren't going to stop erecting houses on vacant lots. All by itself, Mouse Code was only a language for signaling. As you know, most all the field mice had turned against Hannibal. His biggest challenge was convincing the mice and voles and rats and moles – and, for that matter, the garter snakes and blue racers — to join forces. Radio alone couldn't unify the animals against the invaders. I spent a lot of nights listening in on some awfully bad reports from the Rodent Defense Forces, and the Reptile Regiment had its ups and downs, too.

"I'll tell you what," Homer Crouch said. "If you'll come back next Saturday, I'll tell you how Mouse Code helped the field mice trump the corn planters. But before I get started on that, I'll have to tell you how Hannibal Mouse saved the life of my old tomcat – and how my cat in turn saved Arthur Mouse.

"Right now, though, I have to go home to dinner. So tell me — will you come back to hear the rest of my story?"

MORSE AND YOU

Have you ever seen the movie, *The Hunt for Red October*? In a crucial scene, the skipper of a renegade Soviet missile submarine and the captain of a U.S. attack sub talk to each other by flashing lights through their periscopes. What language did they use?

Morse Code!

The U.S. Army and U.S. Coast Guard have abandoned Morse Code. They replaced it with newer forms of communication. The Federal Communications Commission no longer examines radio amateurs in Morse Code proficiency. But the U.S. Navy still trains people to send and receive with Morse. The Navy knows Morse can be useful.

You don't have to be in the Navy to make use of Morse Code. It is a language anyone can learn. But because it's considered outmoded, few people are moved to learn it. That means if YOU take the time to learn Morse Code, YOU will be able to speak and understand a private language. Get your friends and family to learn Morse Code, and you will share a secret lingo that most people won't understand.

Better yet, you can eavesdrop on an area of the world where people still speak and understand Morse Code. That is amateur, or "ham," radio. With a shortwave receiver and an understanding of Morse Code, you can listen to conversations

between hams talking to each other from the house next door maybe, or maybe even from the opposite side of the Earth.

Morse Code has been in use since the 1840s. Operators translated clicks and pauses made by telegraph sounders into English, or whatever language they were using. That first Morse Code is called American Morse. When radio came into use in the 1890s, Morse Code was used, although some characters were changed. The code that came into use for radio is known as International Morse. The sound of Morse over radio is a tone, like a single musical note.

If you sing or play a musical instrument, you probably know that making good music calls for keeping time. If you know how to keep a beat for music, you will have no trouble learning the basics of Morse. If you are not a musician, never fear: You can learn the basic concept of timekeeping for Morse — and turn it to good use if you take up music!

The basic unit of Morse Code is the dot. It is also called a "di" or a "dit," because dit resembles more closely the sound we actually hear. Everything in Morse is based on the length or duration of the dit.

The other sound in Morse is the dot or "dah." The dah lasts three times as long as the dit.

Dits and dahs in a character are separated by a pause lasting the length or duration of one dit.

The letters within a word are separated by a pause lasting the length of three dits or one dah.

Words are separated by a pause equal to seven dits.

To send Morse Code, you will need a "key." A key is really a switch. It turns an electrical circuit on and off. That is really all Morse Code by radio is – a simple switching on and off of a transmitter. Think of the switch on a flashlight. That is a sort of key. It turns the light on and off.

I once made a key out of a piece of tin. I nailed a strip of tin to a board and connected a wire to it. When I pushed the metal down, it hit another piece of tin with another wire attached. The wires led to a battery and a buzzer. The key opened and closed the circuit between the battery, or source of electricity, and the buzzer. Press the tin – I mean, the key – and the buzzer sounded.

Homer Crouch's key is like a British telegraph key I bought in a London flea market. It is big, heavy, and doesn't send very fast. It is called a "straight" key, because you operate it by pushing a lever straight up and down. A really good operator can send Morse at up to 35 words per minute with a straight key.

Because Homer was a railroad telegraph operator, he also used a semiautomatic key, or "bug." A bug makes dots and dashes independently. The dots are generated by a thin metal reed that vibrates when the operator presses a thumb lever. The vibrations make a series of dots. The dot string stops when the operator stops pressing the thumb key. In 1939, Ted McElroy sent Morse at 75.2 words per minute.

Even at 75 words per minute, Morse is a fairly slow way of sending information. When Arthur Vail helped Samuel Morse develop a code in the 1840s, he assigned the shortest sounds to the most common letters. He found that the letter "E" was the most used letter in English, so he assigned it the shortest character — a single dit. The letter "I" is also common. It is di-dit. "A" is di-dah. "U" is di-di-dah. On the other hand, less-used letters got longer sounds. "P" is di-dah-dah-dit. "Q" is dah-dah-di-dah.

The need to speed up transmission led to other ways of shortening words. There is a system of Q signals, for instance. "QTH" means "my location is" such and such a place. If a station says "QRT," it's going off the air.

Does this sound a lot like texting over cell phones? Radio operators might tell someone via Morse, BCNU – be seeing you, or CUL – see you later. If someone tells you 73, it means "best regards."

An OM is Old Man. A YL is a young lady. An XYL or YF is a wife.

It's good to know the international distress signal in Morse. It is SOS, or di-di-dit dah-dah-dah di-di-dit.

You will have to memorize the code. This is easier than it sounds. The best way to memorize the code is to practice sending it. Morse Code keys and practice oscillators (they make the tones) may be purchased over the Internet. In a pinch, you could use an old electric doorbell or buzzer. Want to get started right now, without waiting for a key and a noisemaker? No problem! No equipment needed. You can sing the dits and dahs. Or you can honk them on a car horn – if your neighbors don't object.

Start by sending your name. That way, you will learn a handful of letters, and that will be the foundation from which you increase your knowledge of Morse.

Now, let's have a look at the Morse Code.

Character	Sound	Written
A	di-DAH	._
B	DAH-di-di-dit	_...
C	DAH-di-DAH-dit	_._.
D	Dah-di-dit	_..
E	dit	.
F	di-di-DAH-dit	.._.
G	DAH-DAH-dit	__.
H	di-di-di-dit	....
I	di-dit	..
J	di-DAH-DAH-DAH	.___
K	DAH-di-DAH	_._
L	di-DAH-di-dit	._..
M	DAH-DAH	__
N	DAH-dit	_.
0	DAH-DAH-DAH	___
P	di-DAH-DAH-dit	.__.
Q	DAH-DAH-di-DAH	__._
R	di-DAH-dit	._.
S	di-di-dit	...
T	DAH	_
U	di-di-DAH	.._
V	di-di-di-DAH	..._
W	di-DAH-DAH	.__
X	DAH-di-di-DAH	_.._
Y	DAH-di-DAH-DAH	_.__
Z	DAH-DAH-di-di	__..
1	di-DAH-DAH-DAH-DAH	.____
2	di-di-DAH-DAH-DAH	..___
3	di-di-di-DAH-DAH	...__

Character	Sound	Written
4	di-di-di-di-DAH	...._
5	di-di-di-di-dit	.....
6	DAH-di-di-di-dit	_....
7	DAH-DAH-di-di-dit	_ _...
8	DAH-DAH-DAH-di-dit	_ _ _..
9	DAH-DAH-DAH-DAH-dit	_ _ _ _.
0	DAH-DAH-DAH-DAH-DAH	_ _ _ _ _
Period	di-DAH-di-DAH-di-DAH	._._._
Comma	DAH-DAH-di-di-DAH-DAH	_ _.._ _
Question	di-di-DAH-DAH-di-dit	.._ _..

ABOUT THE AUTHOR

Joel Thurtell learned Morse Code at age 13, when he passed an FCC test and was first licensed to operate an amateur radio station (1959). His call sign is K8PSV.

Joel is the author of *Seydou's Christmas Tree*, a story for young readers from his days as a Peace Corps volunteer in Togo, West Africa.

His book *Up the Rouge!*, about politics, pollution and Detroit's Rouge River, was named a Michigan Notable Book by the Library of Michigan.

Joel earned a B.A. in history at Kalamazoo College and an M.A. in history at the University of Michigan.

He was a reporter for the South Bend Tribune and Detroit Free Press.

He's written about the history of amateur radio for QST, CQ and Electric Radio.

He lives in Plymouth, Michigan, with his wife, Karen Fonde, M.D., and their lapdog, Patti.

ABOUT THE ILLUSTRATOR

John Barnhart received his MFA in painting from Columbia University in 1987. He illustrated his first children's book when he was 15 and has continued to illustrate them ever since.

He regularly exhibits his paintings both here and abroad; he lives and works in Brooklyn, New York.

CPSIA information can be obtained at www.ICGtesting.com
Printed in the USA
BVOW021442260812

298683BV00007B/7/P